For lightness of being . . .

First U.S. edition 2005

Library of Congress Cataloging-in-Publication Data is available.

Library of Congress Catalog Card Number 2003069624

ISBN 0-7636-2549-3

2 4 6 8 10 9 7 5 3

Printed in Singapore

This book was typeset in Berling.
The illustrations were done in colored pencil and pastel.

Candlewick Press
2067 Massachusetts Avenue
Cambridge, Massachusetts 02140

visit us at www.candlewick.com

Here We Go, Harry

Kim Lewis

CANDLEWICK PRESS
CAMBRIDGE, MASSACHUSETTS

There was a little hill near Harry's house.

It wasn't too high. It wasn't too far.

Harry climbed up with his friends, Ted and Lulu.

On the top of the hill, it was windy.

Clouds were floating along in the sky.

Birds were swooping up and down in the air.

"Whoops!" said Harry, as the breeze flapped his ears.

"Wheee!" said Ted, as it tickled his fur.

"Whoopee!" said Lulu, feeling loopy and frisky.

Lulu ran in the grass.

She hopped one, two, three.

She leapt from the hill.

"Look at me, Ted and Harry!" called Lulu.

And she flew in the air as light as could be.

"Wait for me, Lulu!" said Ted.

He ran in the grass. He hopped one, two, three.

"Wheee! Look at me!" cried Ted.

And he flew in the air with the wind from the hill.

"Whoopee!" and "Wheee!" shouted Lulu and Ted,
  as they tumbled down the hill in the soft summer grass.
  They went roly poly all the way to the bottom.
"What about me?" wondered Harry.

Harry peered over the edge of the hill.

His ears flapped this way and that in the wind.

His fur felt ruffled.

His trunk felt tickled.

"Come on, Harry!" called Lulu and Ted.

Harry ran back a little.

He hopped . . . one, two, three.

Then a small puff of wind blew Harry's ears.

Both of them flapped right over his eyes.

Harry stopped on the edge of the hill.

He couldn't take off.

He didn't feel right.

He didn't feel loopy,

or swoopy, or light.

"You can do it, Harry!" called Lulu and Ted.

But Harry just sat there, all by himself.

Lulu and Ted ran back up the hill.

"We'll go with you, Harry," said Ted.

"Ready now, Harry?" said Lulu.

Lulu and Ted held Harry's ears.

They ran in the grass.

They hopped . . . one, two, three.

"Oh, OH!" said Harry. He took a deep breath.

And before Harry knew it, off they all flew.

His ears spread wide in the wind.

He felt as loopy and swoopy and light as could be,

for one long, lovely second.

Then the three little friends landed tumble-slump
and went roly poly in the soft hill grass.

"Whoopee! Wheee! Whoops!" cried Lulu, Ted, and Harry.

"We did it," said Harry. "We did it together!"

And on the little hill near Harry's house,

which wasn't too high and wasn't too far,

Harry, Ted, and Lulu went jumping again.

"Here we go, Harry!" said Lulu and Ted.

And Harry, with his ears spread wide in the wind,

flew the longest and lightest of all.